CH00933064

THE DEATH OF SADIE ROPER

Malcolm Noble has written fourteen full
length mystery novels set in the south of
England from the 1920s to the 1960s.
Press reviews have emphasised his sense
of place and atmosphere, his strong
characterisation and first rate storytelling.
Now, the Goodladies Thriller Library
offers that same excitement in his shorter
fiction.

As a young man, Malcolm Noble served
in the Portsmouth Police, a chapter of
his life that provides some inspiration for
his crime fiction. Malcolm, who has
presented his own weekly book
programme on local radio, now lives in
Market Harborough where he and his
wife run a second-hand bookshop.

1

BY THE SAME AUFHOR

Peggy Pinch Investigates
Peggy Pinch, Policeman's Wife
Murder in a Parish Chest
The Body in the Bicycle Shed*

The Timberdick Mysteries
A Mystery of Cross Women*~
The Case of the Dirty Verger
Timberdick's First Case
Liking Good Jazz
Piggy Tucker's Poison
The Parish of Frayed Ends
The Clue of the Curate's Cushion
The Case of the Naughty Wife
The Poisons of Goodladies Road
Take Seven Cooks (a play)

The Ned Machray Memoirs
The Baker Street Protectors

The Goodladies Thriller Library
#1 Bullet For a Preacher

"Parochial Policing at its Best" (*Shropshire Star*)
malcolmnoble.com

*also available as an e-book
~ out of print

Malcolm Noble

The Death of Sadie Roper
Goodladies Thriller Library

"If you're right, Sadie Roper
is dead, dumb and filthy rich ..."

The Bookcabin
Market Harborough
2015

3

The Goodladies Thriller Library is published at
The Bookcabin
7-9 Coventry Road, Market Harborough LE16 9BX

The Death of Sadie Roper

Copyright © 2015 Malcolm Noble
The moral right of the author has been asserted.

Apart from fair dealing for the purposes of research or private study, or criticism or review, permitted under the Copyright, Designs and Patents Act 1988, this publication may only be reproduced, stored or transmitted, in any form or means, with the prior permission in writing of the publisher, or in the case of reprographic reproduction in accordance with the terms of licences issued by the Copyright Licensing Agency. Enquiries concerning reproduction outside those terms should be sent to the publishers.

This is a work of fiction. All persons and events are imaginary and any resemblance to actual persons and events is purely coincidental.

ISBN 978-0-9932700-0-0

The Death of Sadie Roper
by Malcolm Noble

At two that morning, I washed the curry plates and left the CoOp furniture store in the hands of the night-watchman. I crossed Goodladies Road at the junction with Eversley and made my way through the bent alley between the garrets of the old shipping quarter. Two lads, camping on the wrought iron footbridge for the night, train-spotting, had told me that an old man with a handcart had been wheeling rubbish from the back of the Hoboken Arms to None Nicer Yard and I thought I would take a look. Once upon a time it had been Neugneiser but the locals couldn't manage that so they pinched the slogan from Three Nuns tobacco and called it None Nicer. Three dead ends of falling down houses between the backs of Eversley and the five ways junction (they weren't grand enough to be called slums) used it as a rubbish plot. Every three months, the smell reached the council depot and they sent a front loading tipper to shovel up the worst of it.

It was black. The high walls kept the moonlight away and I had to use my policeman's torch. The wet brick walls were grey with grime; the old cobbles, slippery with slime. I didn't want to touch the walls so I trod forward, half a step at a time, like a toddler on his first steps. The cats had got there before me but something was wrong. They were tugging at the clothes and sacks but the smell stopped them from wrestling with them. They drew back so that I could have a go. The Guildhall clock struck the quarter hour and the mechanics who had been working on a disabled trolleybus, abandoned on Goodladies Road since eleven, managed to get it going again. The lads on the bridge hadn't seen a train in thirty minutes. Somewhere, a locked out husband was banging on his front door and the last of the ferry boats would be tying up. The cats didn't take their eyes off me. If there had been any light, cats' eyes would have sparkled at me. I felt like the fall guy. When I toed a boot into the pile of rags, the stench threw me back against the wall.

Argylle called up his biggest patrol car and told the driver to sit with his headlights beaming down the alley. That was enough to draw a crowd, even in the middle of the night. People had put overcoats and jackets over their nightclothes; half were in slippers. One of the women at the upstairs windows shouted, "Which one have you got, Ned?" another, "What have they done to her?" But we had no trouble keeping them away from the None Nicer Yard; they lined the opposite pavement and someone spoke about opening the chip shop.

The doctor had been down there for three quarters of an hour.

I stayed in the middle of the road, not wanting to talk with the spectators until I was sure what we were in the middle of. I heard the freight train rattle over the viaduct and remembered the lads on the footbridge. I tagged a probationer and told him to bring them to the main road. Unlucky things happen to witnesses in a murder case.

Argylle came out of the darkness of the yard and asked what I'd been eating.

"Sorry, gov. Singers curry with an old Chindit from the CoOp."

"You've damned well sprayed the crime scene, Machray."

"I was throwing up before I knew it, sir."

He shook his head. "An old hand like you."

We turned our attention to the doctor. He was wearing a Russian hat pulled down over his ears, a scarf comforting his throat, a Kashmir overcoat and brown brogues. He looked like a doctor who only dealt with clean bodies.

"You'll move her with a light touch, I'm sure. Warn your lads that she'll come apart. Remember the poor mortician. He'll want as much to work with as you can give him."

"I'll trust it to my best men, doctor."

"I'm off to bed," he said, straightening his posh leather gloves over the backs of his hands. "Next time, constable, you'll do us all the courtesy of vomiting in the gutter?"

This was going to take some living down. Both gentlemen were grinning like pompous prefects.

Doctor Mortimer said, "She's been there - oh, I don't know - probably no longer than four or five days. The flesh would decompose very easily in those conditions. How much shall I say? You're looking for a killer."

The superintendent sort of snorted. We knew that much.

"I mean an expert. One clean shot through the back of her neck. Nearly took the head off but left her brains pretty much intact. He knew what he was doing. But, curiously ..."

"Yes?"

"She's the victim of an old crime. Years ago, someone who didn't know how to do it, cut out her tongue."

That stalled any cleverness from Superintendent Argylle. "You mean?"

"I mean someone who didn't know how to do it, tore her tongue out."

"God help her," I breathed.

The photographer turned up in his A35 van, police blue, and Argylle sent him to work. The dog handlers were in a huddle outside the Hoboken Arms. A brace of detectives were writing things down but kept away from the alley. No one wanted to get close to this corpse. "The chief will have to bring in the Met," Argylle mumbled. "We all know how he'll feel about that." He looked to me. "You're going to tell me that you've got no mutes on Goodladies Road?"

"That much, I can promise. But we've got the report of a man with a handcart. I'll look into that."

"You know he'll have nothing to tell us. God, Ned, you sound like we're clutching at straws from the start."

The folk in pyjamas were keen to guess her identity. Someone spoke of an old woman who kept cats in Beckersby Woods and Ma Shipley was telling Mrs Harkness that Drew Roberts hadn't been seen in a fortnight. But Drew had a tongue in her head; I didn't know anything about the cat-woman.

Smithers marched forward from the kerb and offered Argylle his hand. "Constable Ned will tell you who I am, wing-co."

"Chief superintendent," the governor corrected.

"Smithers, East Lancs Air Dispatch, end of '43. Commander, I want to say this looks like a woman's job to me. Clean, neat, no more damage than necessary, and those blankets - she was trying to make the body comfortable rather than hiding it." He was on the button but we took no notice.

"Put yourself about," said the boss, " and I'll rattle off a telex for anyone who's missing and can't talk about it." He was ready to walk away from the mess. "Something will turn up."

But his trawl produced no reports and within a week the None Nicer corpse had begun to look like a cold case. Then, when I was off duty and in Alf's cafe, waiting for the rain to stop, Ma Shipley came in with a huge dog that tried to sit beneath her table but took up most of her aisle.

"Good god, Ma. She's filthy."

"She's been in the swamp. Lord knows what I'm to do with her." Ma was a broad beamed heavyweight who was always trying to manage her bust.

"Ma, please," Alf shouted from the counter. "Please, you leave her outside."

"I'm here for your bubble and squeak, Alf Martins, and I'll take it without your complainings. Ned, I haven't told you before because, well, there's hardly anything to say. But it seems to me that a woman with her tongue out is a rare thing. I mean, you just don't hear of it twice in one lifetime." The dog groaned and the table legs moved. Ma pushed herself back and sat with her plump knees open and the hound settled between her feet.

Alf's daughter brought my Wednesday Special from the back kitchen and left a gingham napkin for me to mop up with. "Soapy says that Jack Williams has got a ride in the three-forty at Fontwell. Otherwise, it's trap six in the last race at the dogs tonight. Dad's new bird wants to know what you think."

"Tell her to leave both alone. Soapy's in the middle of a bad patch."

When we were alone, I edged my chair closer to Ma's table. "Who's the new bird?"

"Angel Withers from Eversley Street," she confided, very quietly. "She threw her old man out last week so that she could move in here." She spilled half her tea into a saucer and, with all the difficulty of an ample woman, laid it on the floor for the dog.

"No, Ma! Please! Think of my customers!"

"Here's what I've got," she said, lighting a fresh cigarette from the tip of one in her mouth. "Years ago. I'm talking before I was thirty. I had a punter from the docks. One of the foreigns, but clean and ever so polite. You know what things were like in those days." She coughed rudely.

I was busy with the arithmetic and guessed she was speaking about the late 1920s, although Ma was a woman who would have spent a long time in her twenties.

"He paid me in stockings. Four pairs. And all he wanted to do was bury his head in my flopsies. I did it for him beneath the windows of Wick's bakery. Of course, that was before they put in the new lighting. He had long curly hair, I remember. I was finding bits of it in all sorts of places for days after."

There was no point trying to hurry Ma Shipley. She had a story to tell and was going to reach the nub of it in her own way.

"Things were different round Goodladies in those days. People in houses didn't want working women on their streets. There was only half a dozen of us and we used to work from rooms down the alleys. Like cribs, they were. If we left the doors open, the lads knew we were up for business. That's how it worked. Of course, the pubs and the backs of the picture houses were there. I'm not saying they weren't. They've always been the same."

Other people told it differently but I didn't interrupt. I took the pepper pot from the table behind me and spiced up the hotpot. It was good, with thick gravy but too little meat to call it a stew.

"Only, he knew a bloke who'd heard it."

"Heard what, Ma?" A slither of swede skin had caught between my teeth. I poked it with the nail of my little finger. The dog was looking up, hoping for another saucer of tea.

"Heard them cutting the woman's tongue out. Of course, it could have been another girl but it's not likely. Not likely at all. I've mentioned it to Mrs Harkness and she said, how many times are you going to hear such a story? I mean, you don't, do you?"

I said, with my mouth full. "You're going to have to tell me the story from the beginning, Ma. Come on, give me the time, date and place stated."

"I owed Copper Knott fifteen quid, so that would be after the General Strike because he weren't posted here before then. I'll tell you this, the papers were full of that boxing match because that's what the foreign spoke about." Then a stray memory lit up her face: "I could tell you something else about him but it's nothing to do with what you want to hear. Shelley Goodyear - she who married that sergeant special and spent eight months in Holloway for messing with the streetlamps - was upstairs in bed, no more than a kid, you see, so she might have heard what he said. You can ask her. Her daughter's in Eversley and she'll know her ma's address. There's good collobaration for you."

I smiled at her mixed up word. "You mean, the Dempsey-Tunney fight? Tunney went down for fifteen seconds but the referee didn't start the count. It was very unfair."

"He said he'd been drinking the night before with an artificer who heard it going on between Fortunes and the back of the Admiral Nore - a woman tied to a chair and screaming like a horse while they did it."

"Like a horse?"

"That's what he said. They paint good pictures, these foreigns."

Alf marched up to the table, ready to throw us out. I gave him five bob and ordered two puddings, a large pot of tea and something for the dog. "She comes in here and takes over," he grumbled.

"Taking over or not, Alf Martins, I've been coming in here longer than you have." The three of us knew that he had no chance of dislodging the woman's settled sit-upon until she was ready.

"Who was doing it, Ma? Gangsters, young thugs, strangers? Come on, family? Did they want money?"

She was thinking hard. "It's something you'd do to teach a girl a lesson, isn't it. But, here, there's this. Crike, Ned, you're asking me to go back thirty years and who really listens when a bloke's done no more than pass you a few bob."

"There's this, you said. What's this?" I prompted.

"He said that the knife was one she used for slitting cod. What's that tell you?"

"The victim's knife or the ..."

"She used, I said. Yes, he definitely said, she used. You're looking for a woman, Mr Ned."

The next day, I got into the station early so that I could chat with the station sergeant before my parade. "What do you know about the Mill Street Bank Raid, skipper."

He was walking around the front office, going through a sheaf of leave sheets. "Kirtle Bride's writing a book about it," he said idly. "Mind, she's been at it for four years that I know and she's no nearer finishing it."

"28 September 1927," I said. "The morning after the Tunney fight."

"Probably. Around then." He lifted his eyes. "What are you up to, Ned?"

I told him Ma Shipley's story and said it might help identify the None Nicer Corpse.

I didn't know that Argylle was in the telex room and able to overhear. He walked into the front office and said, "She's Sadie Roper. At least, that's what the inspector from the Yard is telling me. She was the cat-woman of Beckersby Woods. She was a recluse, didn't say a word and hasn't been seen for a week. She's our first promising lead. The Met lads are going through her house in Larkspur Avenue this afternoon. The neighbours say it's in one hell of a state. Do you want to take a look? Tell your muster sergeant that I'd like you to."

As I made my way to the parade room, he called, "And give C.I.D. what you've got on that bank raid. Any detection's a good one, P.C. Machray. Thirty years old or not."

Larkspur Avenue was off my beat. It was good at one end but as I walked around the bend towards Number 135, the road became a hotch-potch of neglected railway cottages and bungalows with peculiar closes, here and there, that made the numbering unfathomable. Gardens were overgrown, stray dogs patrolled like lost wolves in a wrong place and cars with deflated tyres and doors hanging off rotted at the kerbside. The place was overshadowed by a steep embankment, where six railway lines got ready to cross the swamp of creeks and scrap yards. A toddler on a trike, pushing himself along without pedals, got close and enquired, "You ain't from round here, mister." But he was on his own. The big kids thought this end of the road was too played out for adventuring (which was a good measure of how sorry the place was). Beckersby Woods was on the other side of the tracks and nothing to do with our police division.

By the time I got there, the London lads had decided that there was nothing in the house for them. Two were kicking a can around the back yard while another was making friends with three cats at the back door step. A W.D.C. was standing at the kitchen sink, opening letters that she'd found on the front mat. "There's nothing here for us," their sergeant repeated as he went from room to room for a last time.

The corpse with no tongue had lived in a house of old curtains, no carpets and no lightshades. The few sticks of furniture looked abandoned, as if they had given up hope of finding their proper place in this home. It was all for the cats and smelled like it.

I said, "The house has been swept through, quite recently. In the last couple of days, I'd say," but no one was interested.

The sergeant tried to show some leadership. "Don't waste time on that, Doris, if it's just bills and circulars. Come on, let's go."

I looked over the woman's shoulder. "When did she stop opening her letters?"

"Eight days before the murder," she said, "and nothing has been delivered since the 21st."

He poked his head through the back door and summoned his troops. He said to me, "Are you going to wait here for the R.S.P.C.A? They said they wouldn't be long."

"That's got the ring of my sort of job."

No mail since the 21st? That sounded like a good reason to talk to the neighbours. The codger next door had laid out his garden like a council allotment with vegetables growing each side of a path down the middle and a tar coated hut at the bottom for sitting in.

He was standing at the water butt, cleaning his tools. "They don't like working away from home. Hackingborough says it's always the same with the Met."

"You know Jimmy?"

He nodded. "What do you want from me, sir?"

"You've been taking in her mail?"

He straightened his back and surveyed the row of tools along the fence. He took a dead pipe from the stretched pocket of his old jacket and placed it in the side of his mouth before looking up at the clouds and drawing in breath. "That's what me and the postie thought was best. There's only one what's important. It's from Bald Eagle."

"The solicitor?"

"That's right. You've been round here a long time, I see. The solicitor what employs Hackingborough."

"The private detective."

"Enquiries and Observations is what he prefers." He checked again for signs of rain and decided. "You and me, we'll have Bovril in the den."

So we trudged down the narrow path. He was explaining, over his shoulder, "She's come into money, your dead woman. Except, if she can't be found or she's already dead - 'already' which is something you'll need to sort out - in which case the fortune goes to the family. I can let you have the letter."

"Which family?"

"The Arrowsmiths. The family what Bald Eagle's working for."

The drizzle started as we reached the bottom of the garden. I bent my shoulder to step into the den. It was only meant for one and the old boy had to dig deep to come up with a second mug. The kettle was already simmering on the top of the kerosene heater. The legs of the little table were secured with string. Half a dozen pictures were pinned around the shaky wood walls with women sticking their bare bottoms out.

The pipe wobbled between his chipped and tarnished teeth. "I can't say that I was honest with old Jim Hackinborough. I've liked the man for years but it didn't seem right what he wanted."

"He wanted to retrieve the letter?"

He was stirring the Bovril. He nodded. "Working for Bald Eagle as what he is. But, I thought, dead or not dead, this letter seems important, Jack Borrows, and you'd better hang on to it." He started to unpack a pile of small flower pots and brought out the folded letter from half way down. "You see what it says? 'Unless already deceased'. Now, it seems to me that 'already' is an important word. 'Already' before what? Before she was found? Before she claimed her rightful inheritance? It seems to Jack Borrows that it's got to be before the old lady Arrowsmith died and, if Jack Borrows here is right, that makes our Sadie Roper dead, dumb and filthy rich."

The next morning, I was in trap two when Argylle caught me on his morning round of the police station. I thought I'd got away with it but he spotted my boots in the gap at the bottom of the stall.

"What are you doing in my police station, Constable Machray?" He said it with a sense of humour.

"Process, sir."

"Process my eye! I've never seen any process from you. When did you last have any process from Mr Machray, sergeant?"

"1953, super. Obstructing a footpath. I chucked it out. The evidence sounded too much like malicious litigation."

"Get your backside in my office, Machray, and be ready to take notes: Bald Eagle wants to talk."

Bald Eagle had more than his share of crooked clients but his own history was nothing more sinful than bettering our prosecuting inspectors at every hearing. He had made his reputation defending the fly by night dance dens in the thirties and when he represented conscientious objectors during the war, he was seen to favour influential families rather than souls stricken with morals. That earned him credit where credit was important. He had famously challenged the police, at a social function, that lawyers made their money because the police brought cases to court with too many gates left open. In a case properly presented, sufficient evidence to charge should be sufficient to convict. He seemed able to turn every damaging perception to his client's advantage. It wasn't long ago that he had argued that a slow witted D.C. was prejudiced against a suspect because Bald Eagle was representing him. 'He asked for my name and you assumed he was guilty. Isn't that so, constable?' The reply had been enough to wreck the case.

"Mr Argylle, I am here to save your time not to waste it, so I shall come quickly to my point. Some may wish to put forward that my clients might benefit from the sad demise of Sadie Roper."

"The will," I said quietly and earned a sour look from the superintendent; I was here to listen, not to advise.

The lawyer took me to task. "One particular interpretation of Mrs Arrowsmith's will, officer. An interpretation that I might one day be asked to argue in court but I am here, without prejudice to any such proceedings, to demonstrate that such a contention is by the way from your murder enquiry."

And so, he took us through his assembled papers. Each of the Arrowsmith children had alibis which not only could have been easily verified but were remarkably free of any whiff of conspiracy. I paid attention, as best I could, but Argylle soon lost interest. He set his chair sideways to his desk and began to stare out of his third floor window. He had been careful not to order tea and relied on this lack of sustenance weakening the solicitor's will to continue.

"All nonsense!" he blurted when we were alone. "All of it, blasted buggering nonsense. As if the Arrowsmiths were going to do their own dirty work. That's why they employ scoundrels like Bald Eagle and that grubby private eye from your end of town."

"Hackingborough," I said.

"Hackingborough," he confirmed.

"Do you want me to see what I can get out of him?"

By this time, he was walking around the room, his jacket off, his hands loosely in his trouser pockets. "My God, I'd like you to. Every instinct says that's the way forward but this is a Scotland Yard enquiry. As I'm repeatedly reminded, by them and upstairs, Scotland Yard is leading this investigation. I'll ask for a briefing, Ned, first thing tomorrow morning. That will give them an excuse to do nothing in the meantime and I'll give you this evening to run into brother Hackingborough and see what he wants to tell you. But go easy, yes?"

Apart from two teas in the gunsmiths, a fat chip sandwich on Fish Marjie's back step, and an hour on the roof of the old Provincial Bank, I was walking the pavements of Goodladies Road between six o'clock and midnight. The lights of Hackingborough's dingy office were off and sheets of brown paper stopped me peering through the window. I heard him moving about so I pushed a note through the letterbox. After that, I didn't pass his place again and kept to the other side of the road. Timberdick was doing brisk business from her little bit of pavement, opposite the Hoboken Arms while two others of the girls were skylarking at the entrance of Wicks Alley. Enough to put any punter off, I thought, but I was wrong about that. At nine o'clock, I saw Stacey Allnight draw the curtains of an upstairs window in the Hoboken and Morning Glory slipped into an 1100 when it slowed at the junction with Rossington.

Alf Martin and Angel were having their first argument which left his daughter to cope with a cafe full of customers. She closed at ten and, five minutes later, I found her smoking at the bottom of the Rialto's fire escape. "Another hour and you won't be able to sit here for spent johnnies and screwed up knickers," she said. "Did you hear them shouting? I don't know why he doesn't throw her out. Dad and I are all right on our own; we always have been."

"What was it about?" I asked, in case she wanted to tell me.

"He told her what Ma Shipley was telling you about Shelley Goodyear. Shag-Arse knows where she is but won't let on. Says it's none of no-one's business."

"I don't think it matters."

"Dad always wants to do the right thing. It's always been his problem. He says we should all help to keep Goodladies a good place to live."

"Things will look different in the morning."

"It is, isn't it? A good place to live."

Lesley-Louise was a bright girl who took the worst that life could throw at her, and took it well. What she wasn't, was Alf Martin's daughter. In '44 she had been living with her young aunt - a nice girl of twenty-one or two. In those days, she wasn't called Lesley and had no idea of her mother. When they came home from the pictures one night and found their home doodlebugged, they moved in with Alf because the aunt worked in the cafe. There was no relationship between Alf and the woman, so Lesley-Lou wasn't even his step daughter Not by common law or any other law. Things went well until the dawn of D day, when the aunt was run over by an American jeep. It was three years before Welfare took any interest; Alf produced the birth certificate of his own dead daughter and sent the woman packing. The girl had been Lesley-Louise ever since and, like half a dozen similar cases, Goodladies Road adopted her as a thoroughbred citizen.

"I wouldn't work anywhere else," I said.

"Will you walk me home, Mr Ned? We can go round by the trolleys-turn and up past the back of the school." I knew that she was courting a lad from Hestonwurts, the washing machine shop, but it was an on-and-off affair.

A regular driver had parked at the turn and was reading the Evening Post. A Thermos of hot tea and a pack of sandwiches were balanced on his steering wheel. "Why haven't you got married, Mr Ned?"

"Who says I'm not?"

She stopped, looked me in the face and started to laugh. If I had known that was all it would take, I'd have said it back at the Rialto. "I'm fifty-two, pet," I said. "I've plenty of time."

"People say you've got a son who works round here. Is that ..."

"Probably."

She had something of a spring in her step now and I could have left her to make her own way. We could hear the caretaker working late in the secondary modern and she started to tell me how much she had hated her years there. "I'm happy working in the cafe, Mr Ned. Is that wrong? Sometimes I think that I ought to get out. You know, see other things while I can."

She was still explaining how she felt when we reached her back door. Then she stopped in mid sentence, pulled me close, kissed me quickly on the cheek, went crimson and covered her face as she disappeared indoors.

At five to two in the morning, when the navy shore patrols were returning to the dockyard gates and Radio Luxembourg, the Station of the Stars, was ready to go off the air, three gentlemen made themselves comfortable in the three piece suite department on the third floor of the CoOp.

"I've told the woman, time again," said the private detective. "There's no point in writing her book unless she has a theory. No one wants to read about an unsolved crime unless she has an idea to push."

The night-watchman arranged the dishes on a coffee table - £3 19s 11d, but meant for display only. "We've Singapore curry, rice with green peppers and an extra supply of triangular crisps which my Millie fried in her big pan. You won't want extra salt but you've a choice of topping. Sliced banana or parmesan cheese."

The detective was long-legged with lanky arms and curly red hair that grew upwards, like stalks, from his scalp. He insisted on having a short back and sides which made him look even more of a carrot top. When he was playing the private-eye, he covered it up with an old fashioned trilby. "You did the right thing, Mosley, coming back from the East with a Chinese bride." (Fred Mosley's Millie was from the Philippines and had never cooked curry in her life.)

I stretched back in an armchair. "So what do you say about it, Hackinborough?"

"It had to be an existing team - no one could have assembled a new band of robbers and kept it quiet - and since neither of the two local outfits, round that time, were sharp enough to pull off a bank raid, it had to be a London mob. Who'd be interested in a story like that?" He made sure that the dish of large triangular crisps was close to him. "But Kirtle Bride won't listen. She wants to know the truth, she says, and I say, what are you? Some sort of knight errant?"

Mosley the night-watchman, spooned out my share of the curry and passed the dish my way. "You won't want extra salt," he repeated so I spilled most of the parmesan over the top.

"Shelley Goodyear."

Hackinborough held one of the crisps halfway between the dish and his mouth. "What makes you mention her, Ned. Good lord, that's close to home. I could tell you a story about Shelley Goodyear."

I had learned to go carefully with a first taste of Mosley's curry; it could take skin off a man's lip.

"She was drunk on V.J. night and took me behind the Rialto because I was the only bloke she could find without a woman on his arm. I was still in the provost in those days, just weeks from demob, and I was looking for an office. 'You want to make a name for yourself Jack Hackinborough?' she says. 'Go after the gang of women who did the Mill Street bank raid.' Now, that'd be good enough for a book, Ned; what d'you think? Lady gangsters who robbed a bank and got away with it. But she wouldn't tell me more. She'd heard what they'd done to one girl who talked too much. Instead, she said that a bloke from the junction had just gone down for a job he didn't do."

"Jack Borrows," said Mosley and we both looked at him. Fred Mosley wasn't a man who knew much about anything.

The store lights flickered and he went off to check the alarm panel in his office.

"What's he know about it?" Hackinborough sniggered. "Borrows has been a stranger in these parts for years. I don't even know he's in the city. Jack Borrows doing time for someone else? Sound like cocoa to me."

Fred came back, stayed on his feet and finished his curry between us. "Jack Borrows was the only one who got sent down round V.J. night," he explained. "I remember it; my Silve was due a christening and he couldn't be her godfather. Blackmail. But he was guilty alright. He came out of gaol and bought the dead end of Larkspur with the proceeds."

"I don't know about that," the detective insisted. "No one's told me that before."

By the third week of the enquiry our superior officers had run out of patience with the gung-ho approach of the Met boys. "The sergeants wouldn't last five minutes in any nick of ours." "The governor's too close to them; he can't muck it with the boys." Their antics in the police club didn't help but it was their part in the murder of James D Hackinborough, private detective of our parish, which prompted the chief constable to send them home, leaving Argylle to sort out an enquiry that had no thread to it.

At half past eight, keeping out of Millie's way during those hectic two hours as she got ready for work, Fred Mosley contented himself with the back pages of the Daily Herald. He knew that he was the least profitable customer during this breakfast hour so he kept to a small table in the back corner with a cup of tea and two slices of toast. It was drizzling outside and as the condensation blurred the cafe window he was able to see less and less of the road.

I had been told to keep clear of the C.I.D. operation and stationed myself on the opposite pavement on the corner of Goodladies and Little Street, half a dozen paces from Alf's front door. At twenty to nine, Alf's flustered daughter rushed up to me and panted: "I'm sorry about that last night. I wasn't making a pass at you," which made Mrs Harkness turn her head as she was crossing through the busy traffic.

Her face was wet with rain and tiny tufts of tissue paper clung to her mousey hair where she had wiped herself before absconding from the cafe.

"Nonsense," I chuckled. "You don't need to say sorry for that. You kiss lovely and I'm just a lovable policeman."

"Yes," she said, taking a step back and turning, ready to hurry on. "Yes, you are."

"Good morning, Mr Ned," said the barber as he pushed past us. "What you going to do about this traffic? Can't you do a crossing patrol for the locals? Some of us have got shops to open." But he was already too far down the pavement for me to reply with a joke.

The cafe girl said thank you again and ran off, down Little Street. Seconds later, Angel Withers stumbled out the cafe meaning to follow her; she'd been crying and was too angry to talk. But she got the direction wrong and, instead of following the girl into Little Street, she ran up Goodladies Road. "The stroppy minx. You wait till I catch her." People stepped off the kerb to make way and she was still going well when she disappeared into Cardrew Street.

Now, Alf had been left alone with the breakfast rush. I could see him, spitting feathers, and old Fred roused himself from the Herald to help serve at the tables.

Kirtle Bride, our romantic novelist and the now and again researcher into the Mill Street job, was waiting for something to do. She pretended to be interested by the paper shop window. Then she went into the hairdressers and made an appointment for later in the day. Minutes later, she was fingering the veg display on the pavement. When the grocer's wife told her off, she hoisted her umbrella and trod off without complaint. Kirtle Bride wasn't posh but she was too smartly dressed for Goodladies Road. She was all light brown - her shoes, stockings, tailored raincoat and buckled handbag.

The Met boys arrived at nine. A flatbed lorry had to sit in the middle of the road as they made a mess of parking the Consul and an old A35. A soldier, in uniform, manoeuvred his motorcycle past the lorry and three cyclists, on the wrong side of the road, and bounced up to the pavement. I stepped forward, stopped the traffic coming up the road and was ready to help the lorry edge through the jam, when a glare from the D.I. put me back in my place.

Three of them barged into Hackingborough's office, leaving a sentry outside and a driver revving the Ford's engine. When the traffic cleared, I saw the youngest carrying a box of files from the office; the sentry helped him load it into the back of the A35. That wasn't straightforward because the old car was a two-door and they had to fold a front seat forward. By now a cluster of curious neighbours was gathering at Hackingborough's door. We could hear the private-eye arguing, as he tried to stop more filing cabinets being emptied onto his floor. I kept clear as locals called out, "Tain't right!" "What're you doing!" "Leave the bugger alone!" It was too much for the fair haired sentry to deal with. When his colleague emerged with a second box, they were jostled and two of Alf's customers, who had left their breakfasts half eaten, stopped him opening the car door.

When the gunsmith arrived, yelling "Who the bloody hell are you!" he was too angry for me to let things be. I walked twenty yards up the road, stopped the traffic and asked the trolley bus driver to pull across the carriageway. As I crossed the road, I raised a determined hand to halt the oncoming traffic and reached the crowd as one of the detectives stumbled into the gutter. His mate was leaning over the Ford's fender nursing a bruised chin.

"Ladies and gents, come on," I trumpeted. "Let's these lads do their job." Some took a couple of steps back but there still wasn't enough room when the D.I. and his sergeant appeared with Hackingborough under arrest between them. At that moment, Ma's hound came looking for her, a dirty rope lead trailing between her legs, and Lofty Perkins caught my shoulder. "Who's job is it to start the count?" he demanded. "That's what we've got referees for. It was his decision and he didn't count because Dempsey hadn't gone to a neutral corner."

"Not now, Lofty."

"Don't 'not now' me. Were you there? Did you see it?"

"Well, yes, actually." I quickly withdrew the claim. "I was in America and heard it on States' radio." That's the trouble with the fight game. It makes you tell fibs that come back to haunt you. I had never been further abroad than a French beach, and I only got off that because a mad Irishman carried me on his back.

By now, some were shouting for Hackingborough, others for Lofty and a few for me. The Scotland Yarders were caught in the middle. They had to pull back, against the concrete sill of the office window. Ma's dog sat on his haunches and snarled.

There was the crack of gunfire and Hackingborough slumped, blood gushing from his shattered forehead.

"Leave him there!" I shouted.

"Bugger off, plod. He's under arrest."

"He's bloody nothing now! Now, you leave him there - this is a murder scene - and you'll do as I say or I'll arrest you, governor or no governor."

The crowd responded. Stunned by the sight of spilt brains, the men were standing to attention, the women stuck their hands to their hips and, on the far pavement, a child in a pushchair went into hysterics.

I pointed to the gunsmith. "You! Back to your shop. Ring for an ambulance." I looked around. "Mosley? Where's Fred Mosley?" I was sure that he had been one of the first on the pavement, but he had disappeared. So I jabbed a finger at Lofty. "Run into the cafe. Three nines. 'Constable in need of assistance' and don't jumble it up." But the clanging bells of patrol cars were already approaching from across the city.

Billie Elizabeth 'Timberdick' Woodcock tumbled from Ma Shipley's bed at three in the afternoon, caught her naked reflection in the wardrobe mirror and, for the first time of many that day, told herself off for being too bony with knobs on all her corners. "You could hang Christmas decorations on my knobbly bits" was her favourite jibe. "Don't know why they don't call me sparrow legs?" Like a child, she had grazes on her knees and bruises on her elbows. And she could sulk like a child when she wanted.

She went downstairs, collecting Ma's dressing gown half way and wrapping it twice around her. "Square arse," she muttered. "Square arse Timbers."

She dropped herself into the old woman's armchair and sat there until the pot of tea was brought in.

"Shift yourself, Littl'un. We're having a meeting at the back of the chip shop at half past. You, me, young Silve and Mrs Busy-Harkness with Fish Marjie."

"Count me out."

"We can't let this killing carry on when we all know who's done it. Drew Roberts is the only woman round here who can shoot like that. Clean, straight the head. Sharp, that's what Drew Roberts's shooting's like. She was always champion when Borrows had his shooting gallery. The question is, what do we do about her."

"She didn't do it."

"Then, come up with other ideas. Shift, you lazy cow. I've promised we'll be there by twenty past."

"I've got no clothes."

"Yes, you have. They're airing. You can't stand your living outside the Hoboken with grubby what-knots. How long have you been in that bra without washing it? Dirty cow."

"Drew Roberts has got no reason to shoot the cat-woman and her private eye. Fred Mosley's woman's got more motive than her."

"You think Millie did it?"

"No."

"You're good at this stuff, Timbs. We need you there."

"I've got a bloke to see. I've booked him in for an hour before tea."

Bald Eagle kept his back to his visitor and looked down through his office window. "You want to see me," he said, very headmaster-like. He looked a portly figure in his waistcoat and braces and with his scrubbed and shaven head sitting heavy on his shoulders. "But you say you're not in trouble."

I'd like to give you some, Timberdick thought. He'd put her in his broadest chair and she was lost in it. She expected him to leave her alone in the office, pretending he had more important things to do, then his typist would walk in with a list of her court appearances. Every time, he subjected her to this ritual.

"I know who did these murders and I want you to get her off."

"How persistent you people are in misreading the job of a solicitor. I am a professional, Miss Timberdick, and if a client walked in with such a proposal, I must ask them to seek representation elsewhere." He moved to the filing cabinet, produced a garden spray and addressed the pot plant on the window ledge. "Come, little darlings." Then, "Keeping busy, are you?"

"Enough. How would you go about getting someone off with murder?"

"You're sure that this gentleman is guilty?"

At last, he turned to face her and took his position at his desk.

"Bald Eagle, you know that I'm talking about a woman. Don't play games with me. You know as well as I do."

"Do I? Well, let me say this and I can go no further. If you are convinced that this lady committed murder, you must talk to her. Keep talking to her, day after day, until you find some reason to doubt your conviction. Then build on that doubt. Dig into it until you see how it can be justified, until it grows into a reasonable doubt; one that could be argued in court. Consider how the prosecution might question it and keep talking to your suspect until you've got answers to those questions. You see, in a criminal trial we would not have to establish her innocence but inject sufficient doubt in the minds of the jury. I shall, of course, note on your file that I have advised you to pass any information you have to the police. Is that understood?"

"Will you give her a message from me?"

"But Miss Timbers I have no idea who you are talking about and haven't I just suggested that you should speak yourself?"

"She won't listen to me. I'm just a tart who sells her sweet backside on the pavements of Goodladies Road. Dinner times and night times. Sundays especially. Especially, Sunday dinner times."

He risked half a smile. "I shall try to remember."

A polite double knock on the door announced his typist.

"Ah, here we are now, Your file and a worrying list of offences, Miss Timbers, that we have discussed many times." He rose from his chair. "If you'll excuse me, I have matters which I must discuss with my confidential secretary before she goes home. I won't keep you long."

Left alone, Timbers picked up the file. She had only been caught seven times and, with her yen for analysis, drew two conclusions. Firstly, she was very good at talking her way out of a charge once she was in a police station and, secondly, she was very unlucky on Thursdays. She smiled as Bald Eagle's pompous court twittering came to her mind. 'My client presents herself to the bench. A waif in cheap clothing. For a week she'll inherit the dirt.' But the bald old bugger had yet to win her a 'Not Guilty'.

"Time is time, Miss Timbers," he was saying as he came back to this office. "Twenty past five, already. You said you had a message."

"Tell her to leave Mr Ned alone. If she touches him, I'll make sure she swings for three murders."

"You have decided not to talk to her?"

"I told you, she won't listen to me. I'm just a tart who sells her ... "

"Yes, yes. Your sweet arse. I've no time for it, just now."

She caught a flicker, no more than an twitch, in his eye and Timbers realised that her sweet arse could be just what interested the old man.

"All things are possible, Mr Bald Eagle," she said quietly.

He sighed. "I must repeat. I don't know who you are talking about but, yes, I do have a number of clients who might be of - mistaken - interest to the police. Now, anything else?"

He was tidying papers from his desk.

Timbers hesitated.

He looked up from his filing tray. "Take care, Miss Timbers. These are dangerous days and if you know what you're pretending to know, you might know too much."

She got to her feet.

"There's nothing specific you want me to do?" he asked.

"Yes," she said without interrupting her path to his door. "Acknowledge your child."

Kirtle Bride was looking forward to her bed. She waited her turn, stepped down from the 8.43 trolley, then arranged her coat front against the damp weather and walked smartly through the evening lights of Goodladies Junction. Doreen was arranging girdles and all-in-ones in her frock shop window and the young manager of Hestonwurts had left his doors open so that people could hear selections from his pop record department. He wanted to see how it would work; he hoped to do something festive for Christmas. Children, out too late, were hurrying with their parents while other mums and dads were trooping across the road to the Hoboken Arms. The traffic was awful, of course, just as Kirtle Bride's day had been awful. She had spent twenty minutes with her solicitor who promised to write again to the receiver but saw no prospect of Kirtle winning more than a few pence of the missing royalties. She had emerged so exasperated that, although she had promised not to, she had called her agent from a phone box and conducted a shouted but hardly heard conversation about her unfinished book on the Mill Street job. She pictured the old woman, speaking from her cluttered desk, with a fag end in her mouth and a bottle shaking in her hand. Kirtle slammed the phone down when it became obvious that the worn out lush thought she was speaking to another of her authors.

She was twenty paces into Rossington Street when - damn it, she'd forgotten her hair appointment. But all she wanted to do now was take of her shoes and go to the toilet. And, she reflected, undo the bra which had been giving her gip since lunchtime.

"The forecast, dearie," she mimicked as she hung her coat on the hall stand. "We must always consider the forecast." And this idea of yours, the woman had carried on, it's not very good, is it?

"Is it?" Kirtle mocked, looking down at the mat and identifying the post without bothering to stoop. An overdue birthday card from her sister in Derbyshire, something from somebody with their own fancy postmark and another threatening letter from Mr Wilson at the bank. "Is it? Well, you'd hardly know the difference if it was." She added, "Dearie," with delicious emphasis and climbed the narrow stairs to her bedroom. She draped her scarf and cardie over the banister post at the top

Leaving the light off because she always undressed in the dark, she had her dress and shoes off in one movement, then sat on the corner of the mattress as she reached behind to unbuckle her bra.

"Oh, heaven," she said. "You can't dismiss the old crow, Kitty. You've tried for other agents but after fag-end Lil, a writer can't step any lower." She rolled her stockings down, then shook them free and hung them on the wardrobe door to air. She stood on her rug and breathed in to unclip her girdle. Then she breathed in and pressed. Then she wedged herself against the wardrobe, breathed in, pressed and pinched; then pushed the girdle down until, at last, she was free.

Free, but too cold to trot along the landing to the toilet. That could wait, she decided, knowing that her laziness would be repaid with a disturbed night. She said, "In bed before half nine. How glorious!"

She threw back the blankets.

"Aaah!"

Her scream, rather than the surprise, threw her back against the wall.

"What are you doing there! Christ! It's Sparrowlegs!"

Timbers, as nude as the rightful owner of the bed, tried to look coy. She said calmly and with phoney disappointment. "Now, don't play up, Kirtle. Switch on the light so that we can sit together and talk."

Miss Bride stamped her foot. "I will do no such thing!" She pointed to the door, "Out!"

"Switch on the light, Kirtle."

31

"This is preposterous!"

"Switch on the light, Kirtle."

Kirtle tried to make something of Timbers' face; then, as if she had only just recognised that she was naked in front of another woman, tried to cover herself with her hands. She said, "What," then finished in her head, 'is this about?'

She stepped backwards to the door, turned to find the light switch, delicately covering her bottom with one hand because Timbers was watching. The yellow light flickered. She gasped and brought all her fingers to her mouth.

Ma Shipley's creviced face smiled from the half shadows of the corner.

Kirtle began to shake her head. She stepped backwards to sit on the bed, where Timbers, talking to her all the time, crawled behind her, braced her elbows, pushing the woman's bust and face forward. Timbers' boney fingers worked until they had collected enough hair, then pulled Kirtley's head back.

She put her mouth close to her prisoner's ear. "Now, Kitty-Kitty, Ma is going to give you a little slap so that you know we mean what we say. Are you listening?"

"This is that fat fishwife's fault. She's told you I used to slit haddock in her shop on Saturday nights. God, I was fifteen. Fifteen, you stupid bitches. Please, you must let me spend a penny."

"There, see. You're not paying attention, are you?"

"I am. I am. I'll do what you want."

"No, I think a little slap. Better now than later."

Timberdick held the head rigid. Ma Shipley stepped forward, drew her weighty arm back from her shoulders and delivered the blow.

The head snapped to one side, throwing Timbers off balance and onto the floor.

"God, Ma! I said a slap, not a buggering thunderbolt. You've done her! She's out cold. Good God, Ma, get her on

32

her back. Here on the bed. Quick, get some water from the jug."

"Head between her knees," Ma insisted.

"Don't be bloody silly; we'd break her neck."

Kirtle's legs were at all angles as, unconsciously, she tried to fight off the threat. That, and the floppiness of her back, meant that Ma and Timbers had to pick her up before dropping her on the bed. That's when the waters broke.

Before Kirtle came to, the women had sorted their story. Ma was out of the house and securing an alibi with Fish Marjie and Timbers, dressed and borrowing Kirtle's slippers, was in the kitchen. She had cut two thick slices of bread which she was trying to toast without burning beneath the gas grill.

When she heard footsteps on the landing, and forgetting to replace the bread knife, she crept upstairs and found the woman on the toilet. She was leaning forward with her elbows on her knees and her head buried in her hands.

She groaned. Like a poorly child, she groaned and wobbled and tried to reach for things that were beyond her. "Oh God, you silly cow, put the knife down," she said, bleary eyed. "I've wet the bed and I've been sick down the lavatory; what more do you want?" She managed to find the roll of Bronco tissue, broke off three leaves and blew her nose. That sent her dizzy and she would have toppled off the pedestal if Timbers hadn't stood in her way. "How much do you know? Good god, girl, put the knife down before you murder me. You stupid, silly tart. Is that what you want?"

"I know who killed Sadie Roper."

Kirtle was blinking, trying once again to make sense of Timberdick's expression. "It wasn't me. Good lord, I had the best reason to keep her alive." Her face twitched. "I can smell something."

Baker Street Crossword

Here's a crossword for Sherlock Holmes fans to mark the forthcoming publication of The Baker Street Protectors. The answers will be in your next selection from The Goodladies Thriller Library.

Clues Across
1 Christmas over, Sherlockians settle to their own celebration (4,9)
6 Lag's sight on entering Baker Street (9)
8 Homely sight for Norwegian explorer, we suppose? (5)
9 Medium for Carleton Hobbs (5)
10 Wiggins' lot (3.10)
11 A regular habit at the location of White Company's first chapter (5)
13 Was hospitalised Watson reminded of this four tailed butterfly? (5)
14 Following, Reichenbach, a call for the Return of Sherlock Holmes in a near time(9)
15 A cleric's advice on problem solving? (4,3,6)

Clues Down
1 Amusing but slightly awkward clue(3,2,1,7)
2 Investigations, boxed up and filed (5)
3 A Surrey notable (7,6)
4. Expected at the church door (5)
5 Departure point for Terror by Night (6,7)
6 To Nottingham (in search of *1 Across*?) (9)
7 *4 Down* places you on the edge of things (4.5)
12 To absent friends (5)
13 Put Shoscombe Old where it belongs (5)

"The toast." Timbers looked over her shoulder but didn't shift. "Downstairs, I was doing toast."

"Well, get down there! I can't, for God's sake! Do you want to burn my house down!"

Grease had caught fire in the bottom of the pan and flames issued from the grill, with tinder floating across the room. Timbers grabbed a tea towel, soaked and wrung it, then draped it over the top of the burning oven. That would have done the job, but for the laminated poster of the Queen which Kirtle had pinned to the wall. That had collected sufficient oily grime that when it caught fire it sparked and crackled like a premature firework. "Don't call the brigade! We can deal with it!" shouted Timbers. Bare Kirtle Bride was behind her dragging a waste bin towards the back door.

"You break in," she was shouting. "You take my clothes off. You knock me out. Then you burn my kitchen out. Accuse me of murder, good god!"

Timbers was swatting a dishcloth at the flaming poster.

"I didn't take off your clothes."

"You would have done."

"You undressed. Quick, another towel. I've all but done it."

She spun round as Kirtle was dragging the bin across her path. A fragment, its oily coating spluttering and spitting, reached for the ceiling, then dropped onto Kirtle's neck. She yelped, the bin went over and rubbish spilled onto the floor as more flakes of flaming poster floated down from the wall. The women screamed as the rubbish ignited. They bent forward; then an exploding canister threw them backwards and set the ceiling tiles on fire.

"Get out!" Timbers yelled, crawling on the floor and choking on oily smoke. "Keep down! Get out before it comes down on us!" But Kirtle was trying to get into a cupboard. Timbers grabbed her foot and tugged. "Stupid bitch! You think wooden cupboards don't burn. We need to get out!"

It was life and death now. The fire was raging above them. Lumps of fizzing plaster were falling to the floor. Timbers could feel the backs of her thighs beginning to blister. It burned as she tried to keep her eyes open, or held her face up, or drew in breath. Worse, Kirtle was kicking wildly at her. She thought that Timbers was trying to share her hiding place when there was no room.

Skinny Timberdick tried to turn, to crawl away, to fall or roll towards anywhere safe but the kitchen floor was already a patchwork of little bonfires. The wallpaper was alight on the far wall. Everything burned if you moved, burned if you stayed still, burned if you looked at it too long.

In horror, she realised that she wasn't doing anything. Nowhere to go. No plan to try. God, it was only two slices of burning toast and she was going to die.

People were outside. Someone wanted to break the windows, another was saying it would only feed the fire. Timbers wanted to shout to them but no longer had the strength. Breathing was hard labour and painful. She didn't hear the woman running through the hall from the front door or her helpless gasp as she reached the kitchen. Her first hope came when a wet blanket was tossed over her and two firm hands, reaching for any limb, grabbed her neck and pulled. She tried to help, to use her legs or arms but her little body told her that her first job was to cough for air.

Angel Withers got her to the front doorstep. "My old man's a peeping Tom," she explained. "He had his bins on your antics in the bedroom. You're lucky I was there, Timberdick, rowing with him about who gets the bloody poodles."

"Kirtles's still in there, hiding in a cupboard."

Angel beckoned two others from the gathering crowd and sent them to the rescue. "She didn't kill Sadie Roper, you silly whore. She and me and Shelley Goodyear wanted to keep the soft mute alive. She knew where the loot is."

Timbers was trying to choke but was suddenly out of breath and gasping. God, she was frozen. Mrs Harkness ran from the other side of the road with a cup of water. "Firemen are on the way," she announced.

Timbers cradled the cup.

"Thank you would be too much, I suppose" Harkness grumbled.

"Mrs H, come on," Angel pleaded. "The girl can hardly talk."

Two men pushed past with Kirtle's nude body stretched between them. They laid her on the pavement. One of them came back, snatched Timbers' blanket as if she didn't deserve it and covered the limp woman. The two men began to rub some warmth into her.

Angel sat on the step beside Timbers. "Don't worry about this, it will all sort itself out. Kirtle's been saying that her mother took part in the Mill Street job but that's hardly true. She provided them with a bolt hole for an hour, that's all. My ma was old Boddy's lieutenant and Shelley Goodyear's mum drove the getaway van. The money was divvied up and spent years ago but there was jewellery in the deposit boxes. Thousands of pounds worth. Wherever it is, most of it should be mine." She held back a chuckle. "We'll never find it. Boddy Bundle died six months after the job and she told no one where to look."

Timberdick repeated, "I know who killed Sadie and Hackingborough."

"Yes, well, it wasn't one of us."

I'd got the call at the bottom of Goodladies, caught the trolley and was at the junction in time to stop the traffic for the first engine. As I quick marched along Rossington, fifty or more folk were crowded on the kerb. The back of the house was ablaze with flames reaching higher than the neighbouring rooftops. I saw Timbers being led towards Smithers's place; he, formerly of the East Lancs Air Dispatch '43 and now engaged in clearing the pavement for the

WRVS. "Come on, ladies and gents. The ladies will need more room. They'll be here with blankets and tea. Make room."

The tender was still moving when the first of the lads bailed out and grappled to unlock the hoses. The No1 took a position in the middle of the road. He was still shouting directions when three of the crew ran into the house. He saw me and yelled, "Get those houses empty!"

He grabbed a cadet by the shoulder. "Set up a station. Phone for another tender and advise the ambulance, two casualties and be ready for more."

The crew was desperate to get the water flowing and a great shout went up when the jet whipped the hoses into shape.

At half past twelve, dinner time, Billie-Liz - awkward on her feet, her neck hurting and the burns on her shoulders rubbing against her dress - stumbled out of the alley and walked into the middle of Cardrew Street without looking.

"More than enough, was he?" called Mrs Amber. She had her back to Timbers because she was cleaning her downstairs windows and shouting at the girl's reflection. She stepped down two steps, moved the step-up three paces along and climbed up again.

"She will do one day," said Jackie Willis, leaning against the brickwork with his hands in his pockets and nothing to do. "She'll take on someone and come off worst. She's got the face for it, that one." Sometimes Jack Willis was more of an old woman than his neighbour.

'Arry Harris's big truck had already turned right at the junction of Goodladies Road and Timberdick - who had counted seven uncomfortable minutes wedged backwards between the cab seat and its windscreen with her head bent crooked by the roof - was screwing the ten bob notes and loose coins between her pencil thin fingers. She didn't want to cough. Since yesterday's fire, coughing hurt too much.

Mrs Harkness came out of the chippie with her order for four pressed beneath the bust of her buttoned up overcoat. Timbers ran up to her. "I know who did the murders, Mrs H."

"Well, she's no daughter of mine." She shook Timbers' hand from her coat sleeve.

"I think you know too," Timbers insisted, trotting to keep pace. "And I want to get her off."

"Then you're no better than she is."

Timbers got in front and stopped her. "But you want to too. Deep down, you don't want her done for two murders"

"Like I said, she's no daughter of mine."

"But you would have known her. You're the only one left who was living in her street when Sadie Roper's tongue was cut out."

Mrs Harkness pursed her lips until the kissing shape went white. "You and I had better take these chips to the Methodist Porch. We need to sit."

They checked that the heavy wooden door was bolted from the inside then arranged themselves on the stone benches in the half-timbered porch. "Ma Shipley wanted pie and chips, so you can have hers. I can't manage pastry because of my problem. I've a nice piece of haddock and just a handful of chips. Fish Marjie doesn't do you proper vinegar unless you have chips. Angel Withers wanted sausage, 'though what a woman wants with sausages when her fancy man runs a cafe, I don't know. We'll go halves with hers and you can have Amy Amber's scallops. Serve her right for shouting at you." With the open parcels wedged between them, the two women began to pick at the food as they talked, licking salt and grease from their fingers, trying not to touch their hair and keeping awkward bits in by pressing a knuckle to their lips.

"For a start," said Mrs Harkness. "Shelley Goodyear didn't hear what she thought she heard. She was a toddler and let her imagination run away with her. What she heard, was me and Jack Borrows arguing about it. We were carrying on at the time, me and Jack, though he was still living with Boddy Bundle; she who done the bank robbery. So, you see what happened. We knew that Boddy was going to cut out the tongue because Sadie Roper had been bragging too loud; me and Jack were shouting about what to do about it, then Shelley heard some shouting in the street and thought she'd heard it when she hadn't."

Timbers was sucking on a long and bendy chip. "Who did Jack Borrows do time for in '46?"

"That's another of Shelley's stories. Well, it must have been for Boddy mustn't it?" Mrs Harkness took a breath, "Oh, you might as well know. When I heard that Shelley was telling people things like that, I threw her out. Threw her out and she's not been back for years. She wouldn't be here now but her husband's walked out on her. I've told her, 'You're no daughter of mine, so pack your bags and get out of it.' "

Timbers said quietly, "That doesn't make sense, Mrs H. Boddy Bundle died six months after the robbery, years before V.J. night. So much about the Mill Street job doesn't make sense. It's as if people have built a myth all around it and, over the years, everyone believes the myth but no one knows the truth. You see, when you take away all the things that don't make sense, there's very little left that does."

She knew that old Mrs Harkness couldn't reply, so she left her there, with greasy newspapers, pie crusts and fish bones and the monster chips, underdone, at the bottom of the pack.

For a day that ended so badly, breakfast at the rough end of Larkspur Avenue had such a whiff of good humour that Jack Borrows, who normally wore his vest as he wet shaved at the

The Goodladies Thriller Library
Fifty pages of murder, five times a year

Your August/September selection:

Timberdick and the Great Dockyard Spy Scandal of 1908

In preparation:

The Goodladies Thriller Library
Christmas Number
including
Timberdick's Country House Murder
(What else could there be for Christmas?)

This seasonal treat comes at the regular price to subscribers

Malcolm Noble's Crime Fiction
"Parochial Policing at its Best"
(Shropshire Star)

open bathroom window, did it bare-chested. Even when he heard the digger clatter around the bend from the well-kept end, he thought it was good news. He didn't care whether it had come to clear the rubbish, dig out the drains or resurface the road, its chugging engine was a sign that the council had, at last, recognised that the fag-end of Larkspur needed relief. Borrows felt like hanging out the bunting or breaking into some champagne that he had been saving for the occasion. For some reason, he found himself whistling the French national anthem.

But the digger kept coming.

And his whistling slowed until it resembled the noise from a wound down gramophone. By the time the front wheels were through Borrows' front fence, he had taken to swearing.

In nothing but his pyjamas bottoms and slippers with holes in their toes, and with shaving soap on half of his face and the cut throat razor in his opposite hand, he got to his back door steps where Timberdick had adopted that pose that had served her so well on the corners of Goodladies Road.

"I want you," she said, stalling any questions, "to call the police so that I can explain why I am going to dig up your back garden."

"You'll do no such thing." He marched to the front of the digger, the ends on his trousers catching beneath his slippers so that, by the time, he got there, he was beginning to show his builder's bum.

"Mr Borrows!" she called. "Two days ago, I had to set fire to a woman's house before she saw that I was serious. Now, please believe me, you don't want to hear about the ordeal I went through to secure Harry and his digger but, make no mistake, he is going to dig up your back garden."

"It's that woman, isn't it? Has she been saying I molested her? Bloody Kirtle Bride, I wish I'd never set eyes on her.""

43

"Stop wasting time, Borrows. You do know what we are looking for."

"The left over's aren't here! They're in the bloody bank, you stupid cow."

Timbers gave Harry the nod. The heavy wheels scoured the vegetable patch, cracked the crazy paving and broke the banks of Jack Borrow's carefully prepared irrigation ditch. Then it addressed the garden shed, frontally, but from a respectful distance.

There was just a hint of a pause, enough for anyone to change their mind, then the digger's claw rose in the air and smashed through the shed roof. The whole thing gave way and Harry finished it off by driving back and forward over the wreck.

"You're bloody mental, woman" Jack said, when it was all over. (He had watched in silence; it was that unbelievable.) "You need locking up. The rest of us aren't safe."

Timbers looked down at his trousers. "You're showing off, Mr Borrows."

He slipped the knot of his pyjamas, pulled them up tight and tied the cord in a double bow. "I have told you," he said, the words burning on his lips. "There is nothing from the Mill Street job in this garden. The money was spent years ago; the other valuables are in a different bank. Now, if you don't mind, it is very cold out here."

"How long had Boddy been dead before you put the word around that she was the brains behind the job?"

"Woman, I have had enough." He turned his back and trod towards the back door.

"Are you saving it all for Silve?" Timbers shouted.

He turned, frowned, took two steps forwards, then decided that she was bluffing. "A good guess, Timberdick, but not good enough on its own."

"You were down to be Silve's godfather but you were locked up at the time of the christening, doing time for someone else. That's what little Shelley Goodyear heard old Harkness discussing with you, just as she heard about the plan to cut off Sadie Roper's tongue. Come on, why should Fred Mosley want you to play godfather to his daughter?"

"He didn't. It was his wife's idea; the rest you can work out for yourself."

Sunday lunchtime. Timbers was standing on her favourite bit of pavement, opposite the Hoboken Arms, watching the folk go in and out of the pub as she waited to be picked up by one of her Sunday regulars. She was wearing her scuffed white high heels, stockings the colour of rich tea, and a short skirt. She didn't wear knickers when she was working and, although the bra that she'd been wearing all week made her figure look good, she'd left it hanging on the kitchen door handle. Sunday lunchtimes were busy enough without it.

"Old Albert's looking for you," said Mrs Harkness as she waited on the kerb before crossing. "I told him you wouldn't be more than ten minutes."

Old Albert would do for a start, or the young lad from the CoOp who never quite managed what he asked for. And she'd already promised ten minutes for Smithers (formerly of the East Lancs Air Dispatch '43); he wanted a couple of pints first. But Timbers was looking forward to richer pickings later on. At the other end of the street, The Admiral of the Nore had started to do striptease on Sundays and, by two o'clock, when the audience spilled onto the pavements, fired up and ready, there wouldn't be enough girls on the street corners to go round and, for twenty minutes, their prices would double or treble.

Silve was standing in a doorway, close to the junction of Rossington while Stacey Allnight was trying her luck at the wooden gate to the Hoboken's dray yard. A four year old on a trike with broken pedals was pushing her way between the three of them and two girls, a year or two older, were playing

The Baker Street Protectors

A Ned Machray Memoir
on sale 28 August 2015

The unmarked grave of Mr Sherlock Holmes will only be disclosed when a Peeler emerges from the fog with his Victorian lantern held high. Then the true secret behind Conan Doyle's short story The Copper Beeches will be unearthed.

But who is this lone bobby, destined to follow a trail of muddy murders from the dark alleys of Goodladies Junction to the forsaken creeks of the Solent..?

Constable Ned Machray, ostracised following the debacle of his latest secret service, rips the seat from his third pair of uniform trousers in as many days and tumbles into his most perilous investigation.

> *"Death, Constable Machray.*
> *Wicked death lies in store for us."*

In his latest story of crime and confusion, prolific crime writer Malcolm Noble takes us back to 1949, a world of post-war rationing, power cuts and daily smog.

The Baker Street Protectors is an exciting whodunit that will satisfy scholarly Sherlockians as well as the fans of Goodladies Road.

mothers and babies with their dolls and prams. Some lads were playing noisy football at the end of Cardrew Street and, in ones and twos, came up to exchange words with Timbers whenever the ball went out of play. Men and children were called in for their lunch, others came out to fill in the gaps. At one o'clock, Billy Cotton's 'Wakey wakey!' issued from open windows and Sunday's wireless band show got going.

I was making my way up from the gunsmiths, where I had been treated to a roast dinner, and got to the Hoboken as Mrs H came out and sat on the step.

"What's your superintendent thinking?" she asked.

I stood beside her in the doorway and filled my pipe. "He doesn't know what to think. We've sent the Met boys on their way and we're waiting for something to turn up."

I saw Kirtle Bridie walking up Rossington Street. Neighbours were redecorating the house, something that Kirtle was no good at. They had given her five shillings for a lunch in the Hoboken but she was in no hurry. When she reached Goodladies, she stood on the pavement and watched what was going on. She stood on one corner, then another, then chose the doorway of Hestonwurt's shop and lit a cigarette.

"Here comes old Albert," Mrs Harkness said.

If this old lady had led the raid on the Mill Street Bank in '27 and had got away with it for all these years because everyone thought that Boddy Bundle had done it and she was dead in her grave, Timbers wasn't going to spoil that. Well done, Mrs H. And if Silve was due the money because Borrows and the first Mrs Mosley had done things behind the old night-watchman's back, and everyone thought it was Silve's fair inheritance, Timbers wasn't going to say anything to stop it.

From the start, she had been convinced that Silve had murdered Sadie Roper because, like Hackingborough, the woman with no tongue knew too much. But now Timberdick wasn't so sure. A niggling doubt had grown in her mind since the to-do in Borrow's garden. First, she had a feeling that the affair couldn't be properly settled without the truth of Sadie Roper's missing tongue - and Silve was too young to have played any part in that. And then, she considered the two gunshots. One, to the back of Sadie Roper's head, a clean job according to the police surgeon, and another fired from a distance straight into Hackingborough's forehead. Could Silve have done the executions so neatly?

Edie Brown, who had the house on the corner of Goodladies and Rossington, was eating alone in her back kitchen. She had left the front door open and didn't lift her head from her plate when Timbers brought old Albert inside and let him fondle her breasts and backside before doing the best that he could on the staircase. That's five bob towards this week's rent, thought Edie and reached for more OK Sauce. After lunch, she would sit in her front parlour with a neatly laid tray of tea and listen to the band show. Kathy Kaye and old Breasie and a turn from this week's comic. But the better entertainment - and this was why she would adjourn from the kitchen - would be the sound of Mrs Downes middle son trying to get his seven shillings' worth out of Timbers. He had done well last Sunday and Mrs B had high hopes for this week.

It was a snatch of conversation, overhead earlier that morning that had really changed Timbers' mind about the murders.

"It could be years before the little mite gets over it. The doctor says she might never." The young mother had been trying to convince Fish Marjie to open the back of her shop early. "Your scratchings is all I can get my Lucy to take and she's got to eat something. She hasn't slept since she saw that man shot. She screams about it. I don't know what to do, Marjie. There's no pacifying her. That's what these killers don't think about - what it does to people with nought to do with it."

"It needs sorting," Timbers said as she stood on Mrs Brown's front step and straightened old Albert's flies. She sent him on his way and Mr Smithers came out of the Hoboken, dodged the traffic, and marched smartly towards her.

"I was going down the Admiral but it'll be too rowdy."

"Oh, what I've got ready for you is ten times better than you'll see down there. Go on home and I'll be with you before you've properly mixed the custard."

When Mrs Harkness saw Timbers crossing the road towards us, she scurried into the Hoboken. I stepped forward from the doorway and met the cheapest whore on Goodladies Road on the kerb.

"Arrest her," she said.

"Mrs Harkness?"

"Don't be daft, Ned. You'll never get the evidence to charge her, even if we wanted you to. I'm talking about the best shot round here. She cut out Sadie's Ropers tongue, just as Fish Marjie had shown her with fish fillets."

I looked around. "Shelley Goodyear? In the Hoboken Arms, is she?"

"Oh God, you're a dope! That's who I mean!" And she pointed to woman in Hestonwurt's doorway.

Argylle watched the interrogation for forty five minutes, then fished me out of the front office, hung the closed sign on the parade room door and shut us in.

"We'll need more than evidence from your tart, constable." He was due to speak at a social meeting that evening and already had his dress uniform on. He loosened his tie and freed himself from the collar stud. "Motive?"

"She believed the money from the Mill Street job was hers. Roper and Hackinborough were investigating and she feared that they would uncover other claimants."

"Means?"

"The lads are searching her house. I think they'll come up with the gun. If I'm right about the motive, she's got more killing to do. She wouldn't have got rid of it."

"Opportunity?"

"She was on Goodladies Road when both murders were done."

"So were others?" he argued. He was worried. "Bald Eagle has come forward. The girl in the cafe is his daughter and there's a trust fund so that takes out any motive on her part. Borrows says that the tart called Silve knew she was due an inheritance. Of course, we'll argue that she cannot benefit from the proceeds of crime but he clears her as far as a motive for murder is concerned. It's all a bit weak, Mr Machray."

"Give me five minutes with her," I asked.

"What have you got?"

She wore the face of a woman with nowhere to go. Her shoulders had dropped, her hands wrestled between her thighs and her feet were out of her shoes.

I sat at the table, not expecting her to lift her eyes. "We'll find the gun," I said. "It might take us two or three days, but we'll find it." I waited for that thought to settle, then added, "If we don't find the gun, we'll find Shelley Goodyear's body. Hardly seems fair, murdered because of something she heard as a child."

She set her face sideways, as if she were looking out of a window. The detention room had no window.

"Burrows told Timberdick that he molested you."

"Not really."

"Tell me."

"I want a solicitor."

"Tell me, Kit."

"Nothing. He used to stand behind me and put his hands over my shoulders and press himself against my bottom."

"That would be while he was coaching you at his old shooting gallery."

"Could have been."

"People say Drew Roberts was always the champion."

"Do they?"

The detective sergeant, walking around the room, scribbled a note and laid it in front of me.

She said quietly, "He didn't like her. I want a solicitor."

I looked at the sergeant who responded, "I've told her. One's on his way."

"You don't have to say anything. Let me do the talking. Shelley Goodyear's not been seen for a week. We have men searching for her and I'll tell you when we find her. She was living with Harkness and Burrows and heard them arguing about the plan to take out Sadie Roper's tongue. Did they mention your name? Mrs Harkness will tell us. She's keeping quiet now. Well, she would if she planned the Mill Street job. But when she learns that you've murdered her daughter, she'll talk."

Empty teacups were on the table. Teaspoons, an ashtray and a half spent cigarette packet. I tidied them. "God, girl. You were only fourteen."

"I was eighteen. Who told you I was fourteen?"

"No more than a girl and likely to lose your mother's share of the money. So, cutting out Sadie's tongue was one way of pushing yourself forward. Yes, I can see that. It made you part of the reckoning."

"It's all 'mights' and 'maybe'," she said.

I got to my feet. "Until we find Shelley Goodyear."

The infant on her trike told them that the gun was in the telephone box. She'd seen Kirtle take it there, the day after the fire and before the decorators moved in. "It's still a secret," she insisted; her dad had said that she mustn't tell anyone. That was at eleven o'clock and the sergeant in charge of the search for Goodyear called his team in. Police Constable Haynes, six weeks into the job and not allowed out on his own, was the last to hear and hoped to make up ground by tramping along the embankment rather than Goodladies Road. He found the body covered in brambles and thorns; Shelley had been shot through the mouth. Kirtle Bride confessed that she'd done it before the murder of Sadie Roper.

The next day Goodladies Road was busy with traffic and shoppers but the place felt quiet. The greengrocer was setting up his display on the pavement and I stood with him for half an hour. We hardly spoke. By two in the afternoon, Fred Mosley still hadn't gone home following his nightshift. He followed me, twittering, as I crossed the junction. He wanted to know if he and his Millie could be charged with anything. "With what?" I said. "What with, Fed? Go home." Timbers, Stacey, Morning Glory and the others were doing good business but they kept to the backstreets. And old Mrs Harkness, who had masterminded the Mill Street job and got away with it, went about her business in her buttoned up overcoat and black laced boots and wanted to know why the chip shop wasn't open.

Don't miss future numbers for your
The Goodladies Thriller Library

Order your copies from
The Bookcabin, 7-9 Coventry Road
Market Harborough LE16 9BX
malcolm@bookcabin.co.uk